TABLE OF CONTENTS

Nandini and Dolly	2
James and the Otherworld	6
Surbosa	14
A New Friend	20
Master of Pranks	29
Thingy of Thingy	32
We Can Fly	39
Poonam Mentdha	42
Captured	50
The School	64
Youngeta	72
Tower Of The Young	81
THE END	89
All about the author	90

Chapter One

NANDINI AND DOLLY

One morning a girl named Nandini Mentdha was brushing her hair. It was her first day of fifth grade! She was best friends with her neighbor Dolly Mondonek. This was the third year Dolly was in her class. They lived in Bombay, India. Dolly's parents were born in America but she was born in India. Nandini was born in India too. Actually her whole family except her dad were born in India.

Nandini walked down for breakfast. Every first day of school, Nandini and Dolly had dosa and sambar. Dolly liked her dosa without cheese but with potatoes. Nandini liked her dosa just with sambar. After breakfast Nandini and Dolly walked to their school and went to their recess playground. Dolly and Nandini were super excited about Fifth Grade as in the Fifth Grade field trip they get to go to the Taj Mahal! But they can't go unless they give Rs. 700.

At the recess playground, Nandini and Dolly saw their favorite thing, it was a golden merry- go-round with little pictures of Gods on it!

Nandini and Dolly's teacher Mrs. Pareek was the playground teacher for today. "Namastey" said Nandini and Dolly. "Namastey" said Mrs. Pareek. Dolly and Nandini run off to the merry go round. "Wheeeeeeee!" said Nandini while Dolly spins her. Then Nandini spins Dolly. When it is Nandini's turn to get spinned they saw their friend Aarti Tandon. "Hiiiiiiii" said Aarti cheerfully. Dolly spins Nandini and Aarti.

After a great first day at school, in the evening Dolly comes over for a sleepover. They were eating paratha and bhindi for dinner. It was Dolly's favorite! During dinner Nandini's mother tells a story. It was about how she faced a tiger in fifth grade and saved the entire class.

Nandini and Dolly wanted to do something epic too. After everyone finished their dinner, Dolly's parents went to the guest room with Dolly's twin. Wait a minute did I mention earlier that Dolly has a twin named Jennyfer - she likes to tag along with her parents. Dolly went with Nandini. Nandini let Dolly sleep on her bunk bed.

Later both girls were snoring loudly. Something woke them up all of a sudden and they saw a man whose shirt said "James Lamefoot". He said he was King of the World!!! It felt like they were dreaming.

Chapter Two

JAMES AND THE OTHERWORLD

T hey were not in their room anymore! The man was quite old-looking. He told them they are in the "Otherworld" and while they are in the Otherworld time froze in their world. Then he said that they need to go get a Special Map from a library in the otherworld and that will take them to the "Tower of The Young". What was going on? They wondered.

This tower will have Youngeta's (which they can read about in a book called "Youngeta's", in the library) guarding it and the tower has a bottle full of medicine to make him 15 FOREVER!!!! Dolly and Nandini should NOT drink it or they will be 15 forever. Then Dolly the smart one asked "Why should we help you?". For which James angrily said "Without me alive the world would DIE!!".

You know how I said Dolly is the smart one, well Nandini is adventurous and very very very very brave. And the only reason they agreed is they both wanted to do something EPIC like how Nandini's mom saved her classmates. Yes, that might be less epic than saving the world's king from dying, but it is something.

So let me tell you another smart thing Dolly did. "But there is a queen, right?" she asked. "No, sadly the queen was killed. With no warning, a youngeta, her enemy back from high school, killed her. I couldn't save her as I was helping someone else when it happened" said James. "Aren't you sad?" asked Nandini who is smart when it comes to death and life. "Yes, I was devastated." said James. "Oh!" said Dolly who was wondering the same thing.

"Now, you have 25 days. Oh and take this map, it will take you to the library." said James. "What if we meet a demon or something?" asked Dolly. "A demon? Cool!!" said Nandini. She was even more excited about this than the field trip to Taj Mahal. "That's SO not cool!" said Dolly. "You might meet one." said James "No. No. No." said Dolly. "Yes. Yes. Yes." said Nandini at the same time as Dolly. "Now go," said James.

"This is gonna be AWESOME!" said Nandini happily. First Dolly agreed to go, then took it back and then she agreed AGAIN! Then Dolly touched a spot on the map, where they were supposed to go and suddenly that spot glowed and BOOM they were at some place.

But now another spot on the map had a star and they were in another place on the map!!! "Cool" said Dolly. "Yup" agreed Nandini. The two girls thought and thought. They were both thinking the same thing, "How does the map work?" Then Nandini came up with an idea. "We should read about maps in the library!!" she exclaimed. "No. That will not work. We can search about it," Dolly said. "If you have a phone," she added.

Nandini took out her phone but before she could type her password, she asked Dolly "Why can't we read about it in the library?" "Because we need to work the map to get to the library", said Dolly. "You just worked it," pointed out Nandini. "I just pressed it." said Dolly. "True." said Nandini. Nandini typed in her password, 0315 and opened up the app Safari. She typed: How does the otherworld map work? Safari had an answer. The answer was:

> The lucky people who find these maps need to work them. Every time you touch the map it moves five miles forward. Once you get to your destination the map will grow bright blue. Then it will disappear into thin air. When you need this magical map again, just say, "maps oh maps come to me, take me where I desire, come oh come, come to me, I need you I need you please oh please". After that the exact map you wish for will come to you. But, this only works if you have seen an otherworld

map. Oh and of course, they are a myth or a legend as some believe in them while others don't.

"We might be the first and only people to see them!" exclaimed Nandini. "You didn't know they were a legend?" asked Dolly. "Nope" answered Nandini. "Maybe we will find a demon here." said Nandini thoughtfully. "No way!" said Dolly. The two girls spotted a candy shop labeled 'Sweet Tooth'! "OMG!" said Dolly. "I have read about that shop in a book called North America's

Fantasy's. Let's get a snack." said Nandini and she was off, running to "Sweet Tooth".

Dolly quickly checked where they were in the world. Then she remembered it was THE OTHERWORLD! Dolly ran off to the shop as happy as she can be. "Maybe this trip was a good idea after all." she said to herself.

Chapter Three

SURBOSA

Inside the shop the girls found out it was not your regular candy shop! It had candy with eyes and mouths which seemed to be talking to one another. If they were, Dolly and Nandini could not hear whatever they were saying. The shop's walls were a dull gray but the candies were colorful. What surprised them most, was there were no toys like other candy shops. Then all of a sudden, the old looking woman who was looking at them from the counter disappeared to appear somewhere else to put two silent-screaming candies on the shelf with a wicked kind of laugh.

The girls tried to escape, but the old lady who had short hair, a wicked smile and long nails had grabbed Nandini and Dolly. Nandini and Dolly tried to escape but still she grabbed them. She was able to teleport so it was no use. Suddenly her nails dipped into some thingy she was using to hold them and Nandini and Dolly became a candy. They realized that as they transformed into a candy they no longer had the map that James gave them.

The lady who transformed them was not a regular person. "She reminds me of Surbosa, the demon we read about in that fiction Otherworld book - but she was fictional character, not real!" said Nandini. "She is definitely real and evil! I guess she is actually real." said Dolly.

"She goes around turning people into candy and only selling the candy to people she likes. She has the power to teleport and change into forms of other people." squeaked Dolly, when Nandini asked Dolly to tell her more about Surbosa; Nandini had forgotten a lot about her.

When they communicated with each other, they were not speaking english. It was a language they had never heard or said before. Suddenly, Surbosa noticed something on the floor. It was the map, she picked it up and said: "Ugh! Stop whispering secret stuff! I wish I knew Candyanare (the candy language) so I could know your secret plans!"

Nandini and Dolly were able to understand Surbosa perfectly (though Surbosa couldn't understand them). Then Dolly came up with an idea. "We should unwrap ourselves!" she said. They tried and tried.

Surbosa was giving away candy to an older person who looked like her father or uncle. Then both the girls realized what the other candies were doing. They were unwrapping themselves too! Nandini and Dolly realized unwrapping was working and they were happy that soon they would all be free!

Suddenly instead of candies, there were tiny humans on the shelf. Surbosa was disappearing. Then she and her relatives (who were standing there) disappeared. When they did, all the small humans got into their normal size. "Yay!!" cried the candies (now humans). Nandini and Dolly ran outside, hoping not to meet another demon. Well only Dolly was hoping. "That was AWESOME!" shouted Nandini.

Dolly did not think so. Both the girls were wondering why her name was Surbosa and all of a sudden the cars, people and a bunch of other things turned gray.

Chapter Four

A NEW FRIEND

....

"Oh No!" cried Nandini. She and Dolly had read a few books about the otherworld and when this happened, it was a sign of trouble. All of a sudden a big table appeared. A big man next to the table said: "It's the 'magicy' party! Everyone who is not invited, please go to Dreadful Foods shop! Stay safe."

"What is 'Dreadful Foods shop'?" asked Nandini. Another girl overheard Nandini and said "It is a place run by bats and vampires. They give horrible food. As in vampire and bat food! When this festival (the magicy festival) comes, people who are not invited have to go there. Oh and by the way, my name is Lolo Ventinail." "Hi Lolo" said Dolly and Nandini together.

"So where are you all from, I have never seen you before?" asked Lolo. "We are from the Otherworld, your Otherworld," said Nandini. "Our names are Dolly and Nandini. I am Nandini, she's Dolly." Nandini added. Then Dolly lowered her voice and said "But we need some help. We got attacked by a demon and lost our map. Without the map we wont be able to complete our work. We need to get to the enchanted library quickly. Will you help us?"

"Sure I will but first we need to stay in that shop for 2 hours till the festival gets over. Lucky for you, I was heading there too!" said Lolo. The three girls walked to the small shop. Suddenly something was ringing. A high pitched ring. It sounded just like Nandini's phone ring. Nandini took her phone out of her pocket and answered. It was James calling! Nandini and Dolly did not remember getting his phone number. They didn't even know he had a phone. James told her "Call me on this if you ever need help or suggestions". "Ok." replied Nandini and saved his contact number, it was: 3900JAMES. A few minutes later, they entered the shop.

Inside were dreadful looking foods. There were some Human bones with blood dripping all over them (ewwww), chicken bones wrapped with hair (double ewww) and a lot of other disgusting things (ugh! Did Vampires and bats ever, EVER eat normal foods?). A mean looking bat flew over to them. His nostrils had fire coming out of them and blood dripping all over him. He had a blood-colored suit and a black cape. His fangs were poisonous and he had fire breath (not even bats were like normal bats! I can't believe it!). Lolo said "This is Bloodsucker, the vampire who owns this place's bat." "He likes drinking blood," she added.

Dolly was super scared but Nandini was not; she kept asking questions to show she was interested. But an awful thing she did was, she took a hair wrapped bone and ATE IT! "Yum," she said. Dolly, who was trembling, tried it too. She also said "yum". Then Lolo tried it. Even she liked it. Bloodsucker explained that a person who is interested in it will like it and so will her friends.

"This is my kind of place." said Nandini with a huge grin on her face. Bloodsucker asked them to take a seat and he flew off. When he came back, he had 3 glasses with blood colored water and he had a cup of BLOOD for himself. He also had five hair rapped bones and some tomato soup. The spoon looked like a bone and the bowl was blood red like the color of the walls.

So many people were looking at Nandini, Dolly and Lolo with disgust. Suddenly someone looking like Lolo walked over. "Ewwwwww. What are you eating Lolo?" she said. "This is my sister Amanda. And Amanda, I am having tomato soup, hair covered bones and blood colored water," said Lolo. A girl with curly hair unlike Nandini, Dolly, Lolo and Amanda walked over, they had straight hair. "This is Natile Henny." said Amanda. Natile and Amanda walked away with sour looking faces.

A little while later, Bloodsucker said "Did you know that my vampire has enchanted the library closest to here? Well I am warning you that if you go there some books will ah um they ah attack you." "WHAT!" screamed the girls. "It is very true." said Bloodsucker softly, making sure nobody else (Amanda was sitting on a table very close to them, keeping an eye on Lolo) could hear. But, I could tell you which ones." he added. Bloodsucker listed down a bunch of names on a paper with red ink.

- The Ultimate Demon Guide Book

- Bats Vs. Vampires

- The Tower of The Young

- The Otherworld

- Do not trust

"Wait. There is a book about the Otherworld? Oh. Dolly and my world." said Nandini.

"What do you mean?" asked Bloodsucker.

"We live in your Otherworld." said Dolly.

All of a sudden Bloodsucker yelled "ATTACK! OTHERWORLD KIDS! NEAR ME! NEAR ME!"

Lolo quickly grabbed the girls and pulled them over to a closet. Quietly she said "this is a secret tunnel to my house. My house is not very far away, but this will take us quicker."

When Nandini opened it, there were vampire clothes. Lolo pushed a pink cloth and a door appeared. Then, they went through the door and came out in a dark tunnel. "Oh no!" said Dolly. "We left our list!". "No. I have it," said Lolo.

Chapter Five

MASTER OF PRANKS

The three girls climbed a sturdy brick ladder and found themselves in a pretty purple hallway. Lolo asked them why they were in her Otherworld. "We are going to the Tower of the Young to help someone." said Dolly. "I will help!!" said Lolo. "Thanks that's a relief, we barely know our way around this place" said Nandini. Once they reached a black door, the girls were tired and hungry. The hair-bones were NOT filling enough. But when they opened the door, they were in a pretty kitchen.

Lolo started making something and she asked them to sit down. Dolly and Nandini sat down. As soon as they did, they were not tired anymore but were still hungry. Then Lolo yelled "tada!!" she had made a casserole in five minutes. It spelled MAGIC RIGHT?. Dolly's eyes widened. Nandini took a photo. "DELETE THAT!!!!!!!" said Lolo. "Do. Not. Take. A. Photo."

Nandini did as she was told. The three girls headed to the dining table and Dolly and Nandini saw Bloodsucker hovering over the table. He had a vampire with him. Lolo wasn't there.

The vampire started laughing. It pulled off its head and they could see Lolo's face there. "Gotcha!" she exclaimed. Lolo said "I used this costume to make you see Bloodsucker and I was dressed up like Bloodfreak, his vampire." "You tricked us!!" said Dolly. "I am a prankster." said Lolo. "ahh" said Nandini with a sign. There was a clock nearby. It said 11:00pm, they had to sleep. All that bone food was making them sleepy.

Chapter Six

THINGY OF THINGY

In the morning, Lolo and Dolly started studying about the Tower of the Young. They needed to study, it was important. They should know what dangers and bad stuff and thingies they have to use and go through. So they were studying, though Nandini was still in bed. But when Lolo screamed, she woke up.

"To get to the tower, we have to find 5 keys! They each look like a makeup box. With real makeup!" screamed Lolo. That's how Nandini woke up.

When Nandini was downstairs, she saw a blue bowl of cornflakes waiting for her. It had color-changing mini fireworks and when Nandini touched them they were as cold as ice. The milk was the color yellow and the cornflakes were the color brown. Nandini said "well I guess we would have to find the keys.". "How hard could it be?" said Dolly. "Well, actually it would be very hard," said Lolo. "What do you mean?" asked Nandini and Dolly at the exact same time.

"Listen closely. The otherworld is a very very very, dangerous place. You need to understand that we need research and many other things. This is not as simple as your world," said Lolo.

A few minutes after Nandini finished her cereal, Lolo pulled out a research bird - they are special birds that go and get facts for you. Nandini and Dolly loved the colors on the research bird. White, purple, blue, black, pink and red. "Her name is Jelly," said Lolo. It was pretty, just small. "All research birds are like this. Except their name of course." said Lolo.

"In the otherworld, there are different ways to get your facts. We do have laptops, but different kinds. Our laptops are super cool, they are blue and have wings. They have golden wings, glittering with red sparkles. They comes with 3 pairs of wings. They are so so so so so so so so so so so awesome!" Lolo grinned. A few minutes later, they learnt a bad fact. They had to get a chunk of The Moon before they looked for the keys. "A chunk of The Moon! What do we need THAT for?" shouted Dolly.

"It says here that youngeta's need them for making the medicine that makes you stay fifteen years old. That must be the thingy of thingy - " Lolo could not finish her sentence because Nandini asked a question.

"What is the "thingy of thingy?" she asked.

"It is a law in the otherworld where if somebody does a favor for you, you have to return the favor with a gift or something."

"Why do you call it the "thingy of thingy?", asked Nandini.

"Because the actual name is in hindi; the person who made it up was an Indian, named Poonam Mentdha. It is: ehsaan chukana." said Lolo. "RETURN FAVOR!" cried Nandini.

Nandini knew how to understand and speak hindi. "Nandini! Nandini! Mentdha is your last name!" cried Dolly. "That is so so so so so so so so so AWESOME!" cried Lolo and Nandini together.

Nandini quickly took out her phone and went to the Whatsapp app. She found a photo of her great great grandmother, Poonam Mentdha sent to her 7 years back. When she was 7 she was given her phone. When she was 8, her great great grandmother sent it to her. When she was 10, her great great grandmother passed away.

There was a photo of Poonam Mentdha with Nandini's great grandmother, grandmother and mom. There were toddler Nandini and Dolly. Dolly (who has an ipad, that she left at home) has the photo on her ipad. It was a black and white photo with a dog in it. The dog's name was Dia. The photo looked old. All the women were wearing the same thing; a purple dress with a gold design on the skirt and a velvet heart on the top. Nandini and Dolly were wearing blue and red PJ's. But of course, you couldn't see the colors. Still, both the girls remembered the colors on their clothes.

"We might need that photo," said Lolo. "It is a relief you have it." Lolo went to an app on her laptop called research bird. "In this app you see photo's your research bird has sent you. Also, you can get research birds on this app." said Lolo. In Lolo's profile, it showed a picture of Jelly and a bunch of other pictures. One was of "The Tower of the Young."

Later that day, at 2:00 pm, the girls decided to set off to the library.

Chapter Seven

WE CAN FLY

Lolo's house was far, VERY far from the library but Dreadful Foods was not. They really did not want to go through all that fuss again, but they had to. Lolo gave them wings to wear. Lolo was born in the otherworld and she and her family all had gold colored wings. The girls' wings were old-looking but very otherworldly.

Nandini took a pink cloak like Lolo's and Dolly had a cloak the color blue. Then Lolo put makeup on them.

After that, for the final touch, Lolo took a silver brush and brushed their hair. 30 seconds later, Nandini and Dolly's hair was curly and purple. "Every time you come here, you will transform into this costume I gave you." said Lolo. The three girls walked to the kitchen, and went into the tunnel.

Minutes later, they were back at Dreadful Foods. They saw Bloodsucker, sweeping the floor with a vampire ordering around. "Hi Bloodsucker!" said Dolly. "Who are you? Can you see I am doing some work here?" snapped Bloodsucker.

Nandini, Dolly and Lolo started chatting with people. An hour later they walked out of the shop.

"So, how do we fly?" said Dolly in a low whisper. "Just jump and you will take off! Lean right - go right, lean left - go left, stay straight and you fly straight!" said Lolo in a low whisper. The three girls jumped and were automatically in the air!!

"Wheeeeeeeee!" shouted Nandini.

She and the others were soaring through the air!!!!!!!! It was AWESOMELY AWESOME.

Chapter Eight

POONAM MENTDHA

....

Nandini noticed something on a big fluffy white cloud. She directed her wings and seconds later she, Dolly, Lolo were hovering on top of the cloud.

The object on the cloud was an old-looking house; scarlet roof, red door and yellow house. The windows were dusty and the house was dirty. The door had gray and white smudges on it and the roof had 2 holes in it. On the back of the house it said:

To: Nandini Mentdha

From: Poonam Mentdha

Dear Nandini,

I hope you find this letter, I built this house for you. I always knew you would return to the Otherworld on a mission.

I am special, when I passed away, I was still alive. Just not where you live. When you and Dolly return here, you will have a safe house. When you were an itty bitty baby, you, me, your mom, your dad and itty bitty Dolly, came here together - your Otherworld, but you *don't remember as I used my powers to make sure you and Dolly wouldn't remember. I love you and hope to meet you again.*

Love, Poonam Mentdha

"Cool! Let's go in!" said Nandini. "We really should. I think we need more research. Like, this happened so surprisingly. We need to know more." said Dolly worriedly. That's what they did.

Minutes after exploring the house they heard a peck on the door. Then a ding dong. Dolly opened the door to see a beautiful woman; gray hair, pink dress, blue wings, golden cloak, red bow and silver umbrella. Then, Dolly realized it was raining.

Boom! Boom! It was thundering. Next to the rather old woman, was a bird. It was Jelly!!

"Hello. I am Poonam Mentdha. Oh wait! You are Dolly! Oh my!! You look way older than the last time I saw you!" said Poonam. She hugged Dolly.

According to Nandini and Dolly, Poonam was very close to Dolly's great grandmother. "Nani!" said Nandini coming into the scene. "Hello Mrs. Poonam" said Lolo.

"Hello everyone!" said Poonam. "This is my friend Lolo. You must know her already." said Poonam.

Nandini pulled her Nani (grandmother from mom's side) inside. "You must be freezing," she said. "Should I make you some tea?" asked Dolly. "Oh, that's so kind of you Dolly, but I am fine. In fact, I have some books for you and Nandini to add to that bookshelf" said Poonam, nodding to the rusty gold bookshelf. It had dust bunnies all over it. The shelf had a few new and old books in it already, but it only had 6. The books it had were:

- The tower of the young

- Wings VS. Capes

- The lame demon guide

- The wingly mysteries and the haunted house

- The wingly mysteries and the fight between good and bad

- All about the famous Poonam Mentdha

Poonam had brought them:

- The wingly mysteries and the wand of justice

- The ultimate demon guide book

- Bats VS. vampires

- Do not trust…..

- The Otherworld

- Youngeta's (includes a strand of the third youngeta's hair!)

- The wingly mysteries and the frozen person

- The wingly mysteries and the time machine

- Awesome winged dogs and cats

- Winged tiger and lion

- The death stone

- Mentdha family tree of 2010-2020 family members of Poonam Mentdha

- Jokes that will blow your eyeballs out! ❏ Katie Hesshill's bio

- Never trust bats or vampires

Nandini and Poonam carefully put the books in the bookshelf, they realized that all those books filled the bookshelf !! Then an image came to Nandini and Dolly's mind. It was a creepy image. Seconds after the image cleared from their minds they were all asleep. Poonam, Lolo, Dolly and Nandini were ALL ASLEEP.

Chapter Nine

CAPTURED

As their snores filled the room it got hotter and hotter. The door opened very slowly. Bloodsucker and Bloodfreak tiptoed in. Bloodfreak slowly took out a sword looking very much like a wand (it was a sword because it was the material of a sword and was very sharp).

He whispered "choline hemlion," and Dolly, Lolo, Nandini and Poonam were carried away on a fluffy looking cloud. It really wasn't fluffy. Bloodsucker and

Bloodfreak carried them away. Probably an hour later, they reached a blood red and blackish grayish gloomy palace. The guards were vampires and bats (workers from Dreadful Foods), the palace's welcome mat said:

"If you enjoyed reading bats VS. vampires, scram or you will be vampires and bat's food!"

Then, all of a sudden, Nandini, Dolly, Lolo and Poonam woke up. By now, they were handcuffed and pinned to the cloud. The otherworld do have cars, but also many other forms of transport, like clouds, wings, magic carpets and broomsticks. Broomsticks are unpopular, though many people have them just in case. There are still more forms of transport though.

Poonam quickly asked "What are you people doing to us?"

"Oh President Poonam, you don't have to worry, we were inviting you girls for tea." said Bloodsucker sarcastically. "What do you think we are doing? Taking over the world of course!" said Bloodsucker in a less-kinder voice. Sharply Lolo said "Let us out! We have magical powers you know! And Mrs. Poonam and I have wands!"

"Never!! We will take over the world and THAT'S THAT!" cried Bloodsucker.

"Come along Bloodsucker, let them stay in the rain." said Bloodfreak.

"No, I think we should take them inside. If we don't they might use their magic. She spilled it." Bloodsucker said, nodding at Lolo. Lolo became angry. Soon, Bloodsucker and Bloodfreak were arguing so loud they did not hear the girls break free. They used their wings to fly back to the house. It was 11:30 pm when they reached. "That was a close call." said Nandini. "Girls its really late and now that we are safe, let's get some rest and we can make a plan tomorrow," said Poonam. With that, they tucked themself into bed and fell asleep immediately. The whole "taken away" and "getting freed" event was exhausting.

Next morning Lolo wrote a letter to her parents, saying:

Dear Mama and papa,

I am happy to inform you I am super safe. I have 2 new BFFs. Their names are Nandini and Dolly. We are going to research the tower of the young to complete a secret mission given from our great king. I love you so much. You to, Amanda. XOXOXOX. Bye

Love, your daughter and sister Lolo.

"Your handwriting is so messy!" cried Nandini.

"Show me your handwriting! Dolly you too." challenged Lolo.

So, Nandini took a pencil and a paper and wrote:

Nandini Mentdha loves cakes so much!

Then Lolo wrote:

Lolo is a beautiful person. She is from the otherworld!!

Then, Poonam said "I would like to try."

So she wrote:

My name is Poonam Mentdha. I am President of the Otherworld. I love love LOVE ice cream.

Then, Dolly wrote:

I love winning. My name is Dolly. I am BFFs with Nandini. We are the best kids in our class. And we have the best handwriting in our class.

I love gold and silver. And I want to be a farmer when I grow up. I have a cow!

"Nani is the judge." said Nandini.

"I will not tell who wins by the person I love most. I will be honest. So I think Dolly is first place. Nandini is second. Lolo is third. I am last. Lolo's handwriting is rare here. But, mine is very common in both places. Nandini and Dolly's are just pretty. And Nandini, I know you can write small, but it is hard for some to see. I have bad eyesight so it was hard to read. Glasses can not fix that. So I put you in second place." said Poonam.

Everybody clapped loudly. "I must leave you now. If you need me, you just have to say: 'I am a Mentdha and I call for President Poonam. I need your help so I call for you NOW!'" said Poonam. And with that, she was gone.

Dolly picked up the book labeled "Death Stone". She opened it up to the third page. This book was old. The pages were made out of flowers and sand. The pages were sand-colored. She focused on a paragraph. It said:

The death stone is super dangerous. It kills people. Only some know how to use it to bring people back alive. If you hold it, you are dead. You can hold it if you are not touching it directly. The death stone is hidden. There is nothing to help find it. Only great great great Goganggo knows where it is hidden. But there is no known way to find her.

"Jelly! Come here girl!" cried Lolo suddenly. She gave Jelly her letter and told Jelly to send it to her parents and sister. Jelly flew out an open window and set off on her journey.

Lolo picked up the Tower of the Young and opened up to a chapter. There were many pictures. Nandini opened up The Ultimate Demon Guide Book. Nandini read a paragraph out loud. The paragraph said:

Sureb

Sureb is a very bad demon. She breathes fire. Her fire is poisonous. It is deadly. She lives in the Tower of the Young. To get the medicine of fifteen you need to get past her. Only youngeta's can. Sureb makes the medicine. For youngeta's to have some of the medicine they have to give a chunk of the moon or sun. People disguise as youngeta's to get the medicine. Sureb wants all the Mentdha's dead. That is why she ordered a youngeta to kill Queen Mime. The only demon who knows

Queen Mime was a Mentdha, is Sureb. She changed her last name when she and James got married. These are the only facts known about Sureb.

"I do not like the sound of this demon," said Nandini. "But we will need to get past her," she said. "Also Lolo, whose Goganggo?" asked Nandini.

"Goganggo is a dog-like creature with spikes on its back and breaths fire. She has big brown wings with feathers on them." said Lolo. "She is pretty mean."

Suddenly there is a tap on the door. When Nandini opened it, Jelly was waiting there! She had a note. The note said:

Dear Lolo,

Thank you for writing to us. We were super worried. Oh and we are also mad. You missed 2 days of school! Since you are on a secret mission, I hereby declare you will go to school once every week till your mission is over. I am glad you are safe. Please keep writing to us so we won't worry about you. We love you and miss you. Xoxo

-love, your mother and sister

Ps. your father is working at the police instead of the pre-school. Awesome right?

"We'll go to school with you," said Nandini. "Thats a great idea!" said Lolo.

Chapter Ten

THE SCHOOL

....

Next morning the girls prepared for a day at Hills Stoneberry High School (aka HSHS). When they reached the school, Lolo said "I have some uniforms for you. You will get your weekly visitor badge inside".

The girls' uniforms were green shirts, blue skirts with gold dots, a purple hat with a red rose (fake) pinned onto it and a red and green tie. The boots were red with gold dots and the socks were white with laces. The boys wore the same except they had shorts instead of skirts and did not wear a hat. Also they did not have socks. Both girls and boys had a beautiful gold cloak to wear on top of their uniform. In case it rained, the uniforms came with silver umbrellas.

When the girls walked inside they took their badges and went to a bathroom to change. Five minutes later they came out looking beautiful.

When they finished changing it was breakfast time. They found seats on a green table. The seats were silver. Some were gold. The ceiling was a beautiful color-changing ceiling. Every few minutes the color changed!

After five colors, the ceiling turns red for the rest of the breakfast. Then it starts changing again. Breakfast is 30 minutes, so every 10 minutes the colors start changing for another 10 minutes.

Nandini and Dolly ate their breakfast happily, Lolo did not. She did not like what her school served today. It was called Lamgoodpanso. It was a piece of bread with ketchup, mustard, ranch, something purple called gookhoho and egg on it. On the side was bacon. The bacon was topped with cheese and mustard.

After breakfast, the girls set off for their first class. It was a class called 'Study of Magical Animals'. Today, the girls studied Hoposotion. They were tiny balls with red eyes. They had the power to change into any other animal. They have tiny legs for hopping. They speak a language called Hopamriho. They eat ants. Lolo, Nandini and Dolly were in the group where you make their food.

They took bowls and mashed up ants. Then they added tiny tiny pieces of bark. Next they crushed 10 leaves and added it to the bowl. Then they picked up mud with their hands and mushed it in the bowl and mixed it with their hands. Then they took purple worms to add to the mixture. This was a meal completely poisonous to people.

Their professor, Professor Millet came over and clapped his hands. "Your mixture is ready to be warmed! Follow me." said Professor Millet. He took them to a fire that one of the other groups made. "Maira, Sammy and Belina will take over from here. You wait near the Hoposotions to feed them when the mixture is warmed." said Millet. "Madame Boila will teach you how to play with the Hoposotion once the other groups have made the toys," she added.

Madame Boila was the other teacher in their class. When the toys were made, Madame Bolia said "Now with these tiny balls all you have to do is keep throwing them and your Hoposotion, Elia will catch them and drop them in your hands. You try it, Lolo." Lolo threw the balls, Elia caught them. Minutes later the girls were taking turns throwing. Then, Belina walked to them with the bowls of food. Lolo dipped her finger in it, and stuck it in front of Elia. She licked Lolo's finger and Lolo kept feeding Elia. Nandini fed Kali and Dolly fed Anlais. It was awesome.

"For homework, I would like you to take your Hoposoition home. Play with them and babysit them. Then, next month return them." said Millet. Then Boila started calling out a list of who takes who. Dolly and Nandini were whispering excitedly so all they heard was (this is all they heard written on the list.):

Allan - Googly

Billy - Chompy

Sorden - Havan

Dolly - Anlais

Nandini - Kali

Jordan - Vevo

Priscilla - Samhi

Sammy - Lacygo

Norven - Shobo

Bo - Eveyly

Even - Acleyjo

Jo- Verna

Ana Lu - Helm

That's all they heard.

Chapter Eleven

YOUNGETA

Their next class was Goddreana. It was Lolo's favorite. To get to the classroom, you have to climb into a treehouse. In Goddreana, you learn history and facts. Famous people and criminals.

Nandini and Dolly had brought The Tower of the Young book from their bookshelf. Their teacher's name was Professor Missy Morgot. All the children called her "Professor Morgot". But Morgot wanted to be called "Madame Morgot". When the three girls had reached the classroom, Morgot said "turn to page 451. Today, we will learn about the Tower of the Young,". When everyone was on that page she read out a paragraph. It said:

The Youngeta's very much dislike their meaning to the world. What do I mean? Great question. Youngeta's think THEY should be respected as much as everyone else.

Youngeta's have a brain the size of a jelly bean. But they are still one of the smartest creatures who roam our beautiful earth. Although they have become bad guys.

They had protected the Tower. Youngeta's were nice creatures - they had ruled us very fairly. Demons, who were enemies of Youngeta's at the time, had to stay in their houses. They just couldn't go somewhere and use there powers on an innocent person. So the Youngeta's made them stay in their homes.

They were fair creatures. But one day when Moleta, a fire demon, sent a fire on the Youngeta's, they turned evil. Their hearts, their eyes, their noses all turned evil. Their smiles and many more body parts. So Moleta ruled them.

One day, Moleta got a child. When the child was thirteen years old, Moleta died. The child was Sureb, a demon ofcourse. She ordered them around all day. Unlike Moleta, who was nice to the Youngeta's, Sureb was mean.

After Morgot was finished reading she said "Class dismissed! By tomorrow, I want a three page report on the Tower of the Young! Each page should be three feet big! If it is not finished, detention awaits!!"

As the girls climbed down the rope ladder, Lolo said "It's my favorite class, NOT teacher. Professor Hornfry is my favorite teacher. He teaches Sameson. Sameson is where you learn to see yours and others future and past. It is next.".

Professor Hornfry's class is full of crystal balls and past chorbys. Chorbys are purple pebbles. They help you see the past. Hornfry was polishing a crystal ball when they walked in. When everyone was settled down, he said "Today we will discover our mysterious future." The way he talked made Nandini feel cold. Nandini had a feeling she wouldn't like this class. "Lolo, would you like to demonstrate?" asked Hornfry. "S-sure!" said Lolo, half excited and half scared. She walked to the front of the room and carefully grabbed a crystal ball. She blinked a bunch of times then widened her eyes and did not blink even once.

Suddenly, mist filled in the crystal ball and an image of the Tower of the Young appeared. There was Dolly and Nandini jumping up and down happily with the Yongeta's. Then the image cleared and the crystal ball stayed still with no more mist. "Professor, I was seeing Nandini and Dolly's future!!" said Lolo. The rest of the class was fun, seeing others' futures and your own future. When the class was over, Nandini said "Well, I'm glad to be out of there."

When their school was done for the day, they flew to their house. When they were inside, Dolly cried "We were whispering excitedly to a girl with blond ponytails who said her name was Ann. She said her dad would sell us a chunk of The Moon!".

Minutes later, there was a knock on the door. Dolly opened the door and said "our chunk of The Moon is here!". The guy handed The Moon, and said "fifty hamloons please." "These are your hamloons." said Lolo coming to the door. "What are hamloons?" asked Nandini once the guy was gone. "Money." said Lolo.

They opened the package and stared at the tiny bit of the Moon. There were THE FIVE KEYS! Nandini said "Tell your mom that you won't go to school for a little while. We have the Tower of the Young to find!". "You need to go without me, I can't miss school anymore, I miss the classes." said Lolo. She handed them the book The Tower of the Young and Nandini realized that the map to the Tower of the Young was inside!!

Dolly waved goodbye and Nandini hugged Lolo. Then Dolly and Nandini said together: "We'll miss you, Lolo! Thanks for all your help! We couldn't have done this without you! Byeee! Maybe YOU can visit us someday!"

Then Nandini touched the map, and they waved one emotional goodbye, and disappeared.

Chapter Twelve

TOWER OF THE YOUNG

They arrived at a shop somewhere in the middle of a dessert. The shop was called: Dorris's Disguises. They walked inside and saw a lady sewing and a man putting disguises everywhere. Kids were playing hide and seek while grownups searched for disguises. Dolly whispered to Nandini "Let's get Youngeta disguises.". A lady overheard them and said "Youngeta's look young. All you need is to look young."

"Are there any young-looking clothes?" asked Nandini. "Sure there are!" said the lady. She took them to a wardrobe and said "Look in here". Then she walked out of the store. Nandini found a red dress and blue cloak and Dolly found a purple skirt, blue shirt and pink cloak. They each went to a bathroom stall and changed. They packed their school cloaks (the ones from HSHS) and normal cloaks (the ones they wear when they are not in HSHS) in purses that Nandini found at the store. Nandini's was gold and Dolly's was silver. They paid with hamloons they found at the bottom of Nandini's purse.

Then, the girls walked out of the store and touched the map. They reached a neighborhood and touched the map again. They wouldn't find anything there. When they reached the next place they used more hamloons to pay for food. Then they touched the map again. They reached a place where they paid a few hamloons for the poor. The next place was literally in the middle of nowhere. The next place was the Tower of the Young. Since this map was from the book, the map placed itself in the book.

The girls puffed themselves up and knocked on the door. They realized they wouldn't need the keys. A youngeta opened up the door and said "Hello fellow Youngeta's." "Hello." said Dolly and Nandini awkwardly.

When they walked in, Dolly said "Can we get some of the medicine?" "Ask Sureb." said the youngeta darkly. The girls found the stairs and climbed and climbed and climbed and climbed. Probably 30 minutes later, they reached the first landing. Then they climbed some more and reached Sureb. "You want the medicine??" she asked. "Give me the Moon chunk, otherwise NO medicine."

They were about to hand the Moon-chunk but their purses fell. The stuff in their bags fell out. Sureb's eyes widened and she screamed "GET THEM NOW! NOW! NOW! OBEY ME!!!". Sureb creeped to the back of them and shot fire from her mouth. Nandini and Dolly ran forward and got as much of the medicine as they could.

But the medicine was boiling hot and they spilled it on the floor. Before they knew, they were already surrounded.

Nandini grabbed the last of the hamloons and threw them on Sureb; they thought the Hamloons were heavy. Who knew the hamloons were so magical unlike money in the real world!! Hamloons made the fire backfire and Sureb was killed by her own power. The fire had caught her.

The youngeta's were suddenly being nice. "You turned us good again!!" they cried happily. "We knew someone could heal the spell that was cast on us!! When they were out of the Tower of the Young, a youngeta who said her name was Iris Hoggy gave them their stuff and a small bottle of the medicine of fifteen.

Then, all of a sudden, Lolo's prediction came true!! They then saw a portal with words carved on it. The portal had chunky fading gold on the edges. It said:

This portal will bring you back to your room! I will take the medicine once you reach your room. I thank you.

-Your friend, James

The girls stepped into the portal while waving goodbye to their new friends. Suddenly, they were in Nandini's bedroom wearing their pj's. Dolly was quivering. Nandini was jumping and whispering - if she yelled, her parents would wake up and ask why they were awake. Then, they would be in BIG trouble.

Well, even BIGGER than going to the other world and saving the king and all that adventure. Suddenly James was there!! He said "Thank You," and took the medicine. He smiled at them and muttered to himself: "These girls are perfect . They would be great in the war." Nandini and Dolly didn't hear though. They only heard: "These girls are perfect. They would be." Unfortunately, they didn't hear anything else. Then he waved goodbye and he was gone.

The girls were exhausted but happy to be back. The girls soon lay down in their beds, yawning. Dolly fell asleep immediately, but Nandini lay in her bed, wondering what other adventures they might do. Soon, when her clock said 1:30 am, she fell fast asleep.

THE END

Thank you for reading this book! I hope you enjoyed it! Wait for my second book - "Nandini Mentdha and The Death Stone!"

-Suhani Tandon

ALL ABOUT THE AUTHOR

My name is Suhani Tandon. I love love LOVE to read books. I started writing books when I was five, but now that I am eight, I want to write a real book. I was eight when I started and finished this book.

I explained a little about the next book in the series "The Death Stone "so you would know more. My favorite books are Harry Potter books. I might have been named Nandini. I just LOVE that name. I think books about the otherworld are really interesting. I want to be an actress or a spy. If I ever become a Spy, I would write about my spy missions and adventures.

I like reading "The Half and Half Dog". It is a great book! I hope my book becomes a movie. If it does, I want to play Nandini. FYI all the hindi words I write in this book are spelled like they are, and are real hindi words.

Made in the USA
Columbia, SC
19 July 2023